BY THE SWORD

A Young Man Meets War

Selene Castrovilla

Illustrations by Bill Farnsworth

CALKINS CREEK

Honesdale, Pennsylvania

Lord, we know what we are, but know not what we may be.

— William Shakespeare

To Lee H. Feldman, for starting me on this journey; to Carolyn P. Yoder, for guiding me through it; and to my angels, Michael and Casey, for graciously sharing their mom with spirits from '76 —*S.C.*

For Allison —*B.F.*

Calkins Creek
An Imprint of Boyds Mills Press, Inc.
815 Church Street
Honesdale, Pennsylvania 18431
Printed in China

Cover and interior design by C. Porter Designs

Illustrations on pages 38, 39, and 40 courtesy of
Dover Publications, Inc.

Library of Congress Cataloging-in-Publication Data

Castrovilla, Selene.
    By the sword : a young man meets war / Selene Castrovilla ; illustrations by Bill Farnsworth.
       p. cm.
    Includes bibliographical references.
    ISBN–13: 978–1–59078–427–3 (hardcover : alk. paper)
    1. Long Island, Battle of, New York, N.Y., 1776—Juvenile literature. 2. Tallmadge, Benjamin, 1754–1835—Juvenile literature. 3. Soldiers—Connecticut—Biography—Juvenile literature. 4. Long Island (N.Y.)—History—Revolution, 1775–1783—Personal narratives—Juvenile literature. 5. United States—History—Revolution, 1775–1783—Personal narratives—Juvenile literature. I. Title.

    E241.L8C37 2006
    973.3'32—dc22
                                                    2006012151

First edition
The text of this book is set in 12-point Caslon.

10 9 8 7 6 5 4 3 2

*The war now put on a very serious aspect,
as independence had been declared, and it seemed no longer
doubtful that the contest on which we had entered must be decided by the sword.*

—Benjamin Tallmadge, describing the days in New York following July 4, 1776,
and leading to the Battle of Long Island

Benjamin Tallmadge was a school headmaster in Weathersfield, Connecticut, when word came of American blood spilled at Lexington and Concord and then at the Battle of Breed's Hill in Massachusetts, in the first battles of the Revolutionary War. Swept up in the wave of outrage and patriotism surging the country, he rode his horse Highlander to Boston, Massachusetts, to see what was happening.

When a friend suggested that he enlist, Benjamin hesitated. He'd intended to study law. But the fight against the British was something monumental. He needed to be a part of it. His conscience wouldn't permit him to stand by.

Benjamin became one of thousands who gave up their careers and dreams to fight for independence. He received his lieutenant's commission on June 20, 1776, and headed to New York to join George Washington's troops and train for battle.

His life would forever be changed on Long Island.

*The Enemy have now landed on Long Island, and the hour is fast approaching,
on which the Honor and Success of this army, and the safety of our bleeding
Country depend. Remember officers and Soldiers, that you are
Freemen, fighting for the blessings of Liberty. . . .*

—George Washington's general orders to his troops, August 23, 1776

BENJAMIN TALLMADGE had never killed before.

The twenty-two-year-old lieutenant had never aimed a musket at a fellowman. He'd never known the dark thoughts now flashing through his head as he steadied his weapon, touching smooth wood and cold steel. He'd never considered how he would feel eye to eye with the enemy, sweat beading under the collar of his uniform, forced to fire or die.

Benjamin's mind fled the fiery battlefield, escaping two months back in time—to June, when he'd joined General Washington's army and started training in New York. He'd been full of high spirits and ambition, eager to take on any service assigned to him. But he hadn't contemplated the sacrifice his conscience would have to make in battle.

Benjamin's thoughts sped forward to his arrival at Brooklyn Ferry just four days ago. He'd crossed the East River with his regiment, preparing to defend Brooklyn against an inevitable British attack. The threat was doubled: the British fleet bobbed menacingly at the mouth of the river, while the British army had amassed at least twenty-five thousand troops across from Brooklyn's west side, on Staten Island. Benjamin's spirits had dropped at this news. The American troops numbered only about ten thousand. He wondered how he and his fellow newly recruited soldiers could stop a well-trained, disciplined army nearly three times their size. How could they even survive?

Now Benjamin's fears were confirmed. The smell of gunpowder and death hung in the air. Cannon smoke stung his eyes. Shrieks came from all sides. Wounded and dying lay around him, battered and bloody. He and the rest of the Americans were surrounded and overwhelmed.

Crraacck! A shot blasted next to him. Highlander, Benjamin's horse, whinnied in terror. Until June he'd carried Benjamin to school every day. Battle was new to him, too. Benjamin patted his neck and whispered soothing words. Highlander calmed, but for how long?

More shots whizzed through the air. Benjamin's arm stiffened as he pointed the musket. Wood pressed into his cheek.

Time to fight back.

Benjamin fired. The weapon kicked into his shoulder. A jolt ran through him. The shot echoed in his head. He yanked the reins and took off on the trembling Highlander, not looking to see if he'd hit anyone.

He didn't wish to tell his father, the Reverend Benjamin Tallmadge, that he'd taken a life.

For now he was spared that confession.

Benjamin continued to fire as he urged Highlander through thick gray haze and over blood-splattered soil. He and the Americans struggled through most of the day, willing to fight to the death.

Many did.

More were captured.

Riddled by loss, the patriots could not hold on.

A drum beat "retreat."

Benjamin solemnly rode Highlander across the scorched battleground. As Highlander walked around mangled bodies, Benjamin thought of families left behind.

They headed west, toward the river, to the protection of Brooklyn Heights. Starting just above the steep hill leading down to the water, trenches had been dug and fortifications had been built to shelter the Americans.

Benjamin looked at Highlander. He wondered if they would really be safe.

Benjamin and his regiment, the Sixth Connecticut Levies, lay in a muddy trench in Brooklyn Heights the rest of the afternoon, alert and waiting. Waiting to hear shoes stomping across the terrain. Waiting to see the gleam of bayonets above red jackets. Waiting for the British army to finish them off. A helpless feeling sank into Benjamin's bones. After the trouncing the British had given them, what chance did he and the other devastated soldiers have?

Into the night they waited.

The British were camped a mile and a half away, resting and digging trenches. Benjamin didn't understand why they weren't attacking.

The British didn't move in that night, but storm clouds did.

Heavy rains fell for two days and two nights.

The British would have trouble attacking.

The Americans would have trouble defending.

Gunpowder was saturated and ruined. Benjamin lay over his musket to keep it dry. He thought of Highlander. He'd left him tied to a post a few yards back from the trench. Was he all right?

With no tents, no cover whatsoever, Benjamin and his regiment were soaked. Water filled the trenches, at times waist-deep. Benjamin was coated in wet, gritty mud; he could even taste it.

The food and drink supply was scarce; cooking, impossible. Benjamin bit into rations of stale crackers and raw pork.

But worries about meals were second to worries about safety. Benjamin and his comrades shivered in the chilling rains, never knowing if the redcoats would storm in. Was it thunder booming, or cannons? Each time the sound struck, it jolted Benjamin's heart. He stroked the chilling wet steel by his side and shuddered. His sword's razor tip would be of little use against a speeding cannonball.

On the evening of the twenty-ninth, the troops were stirring.

Benjamin caught whispers of what was happening. General Washington was attempting to send his men to safety on ten flat-bottomed boats. But the British army was not the Americans' only worry. There was also the British fleet, still lurking at the entrance to the river. The ships had been held back from battle by winds and heavy rains. If the weather cleared, they'd sail up and crush the Americans from behind.

The only chance the patriots had would be to cross the long mile back to New York first. Now. Even despite the weather.

With the hope of escape, Benjamin's wilted morale revived. He prayed there would be time to evacuate the entire army.

One by one, soldiers left their positions in the entrenchment. In silence, they crept off in the night toward the water.

The Sixth Connecticut Levies were assigned to the one-thousand-man rear guard. Their job was to stay until the end, to watch for the British and to fool them into believing all the Americans were still there. As men climbed out, Benjamin and the remaining troops spread, filling out the gaps along the trenches.

British suspicions could not be raised. If they knew of the move, they would swiftly defeat it.

Having scarcely slept the two nights before, Benjamin felt almost ready to drop. But his spirit would not allow that. His anxiety helped him focus as he stood watch in the deep dark. Though the rain stopped around midnight, the weather still helped the American effort, providing a cloud cover over the moon.

Hours passed as men hauled themselves up and slipped off.

Dawn approached.

Benjamin waited in the trenches with his regiment.

A vein in his neck throbbed so hard he thought it would explode. He wondered, how could they ever get away unnoticed?

Nature was now firmly on the side of the American cause. A fog rolled in. Benjamin could not see six yards ahead of him.

Neither could the British—for the moment.

Soon after sunrise the entire rear guard was summoned by Alexander Scammell, Washington's aide. Benjamin heard Major-General Mifflin, head of the rear guard, question Scammell. Could Washington really want the trenches abandoned so soon? Perhaps Washington had requested only one regiment? Insisting that every man come, Scammell set off.

Out of the hole at last, Benjamin untied Highlander's reins. He led his horse away, near the end of the line.

Halfway down to the river, Scammell, red-faced and out of breath, met them. He'd made a mistake, he admitted. Washington was in a fury. Guards were still needed at the trenches. They had to go back, and fast!

Back in the muck again, Benjamin's heart thumped. He willed his body to stop shaking and pressed his musket to his chest. His fate depended on the weather. He thought, would the fog last?

Finally, Benjamin was told to climb from the trench. He again retrieved Highlander. He led him downhill, toward the water and Brooklyn Ferry.

Had it only been a week since they'd landed there?

It seemed a lifetime ago.

The boats were not back from New York. Benjamin tied Highlander to a post. He followed his regiment and was swallowed into the waiting throngs. A murmur went through the crowd. General Washington was on the stairs, overseeing the withdrawal.

Whispers passed through.

The boats had arrived.

Benjamin was swept into the tangled crush of moving bodies. It felt tight, as if someone had roped them and was tugging them in. He couldn't see where they were headed. They moved down a slope. He fell against the edge of a long boat, already packed. The crowd pressed against him, urging him in.

The boat embarked. It sank to about three inches out of the water. Rowing off, Benjamin thought he caught a glimpse of Washington on his horse. The fleeting sight stirred a troubling sensation inside Benjamin's head, but he couldn't think why.

The fog remained.

The morning was still; the current, rapid.

The cloth-covered oars made faint sloshes as they broke through the swift-moving water.

His mind in a whirl, Benjamin watched the ferry disappear into blurry gray. Again came the nagging feeling that something was wrong.

A horse whinnied from a nearby flat-bottomed boat.

Good God.

He remembered.

He'd left poor Highlander behind!

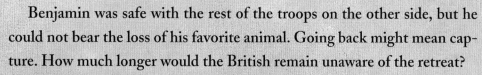

Benjamin was safe with the rest of the troops on the other side, but he could not bear the loss of his favorite animal. Going back might mean capture. How much longer would the British remain unaware of the retreat?

Highlander was worth the risk.

Benjamin rushed to Colonel John Chester, his commanding officer, and blurted his request. He wished permission to return to Brooklyn Ferry and retrieve his horse.

Horses were in short supply. Benjamin's services were not immediately required by Chester. Permission was granted.

With a band of volunteers rowing, Benjamin guided a flat-bottomed boat out. Back across the murky mile.

Back to danger.

Oars slapped water in determined rhythm.

No one spoke.

Benjamin willed the boat to go faster, faster. The misty smell clogged his worried mind. Questions filtered through. Had the British already captured Highlander? Would their boat be greeted by drawn swords? Would they even make it to shore? At any moment a cannonball might rip through the boat's side.

At last, the boat hit the sandy landing.

There were no redcoats waiting.

No pointed muskets.

Benjamin peered. He didn't see any signs of life. He and his men hauled the boat up. He raced up the slope to the ferry.

Highlander stood waiting, alone.

Benjamin grappled with Highlander's tied reins. The beat of hundreds of feet marching down the hill told him to hurry.

Thud, thud.

Soles struck muddy earth.

Thump, thump.

Closer, closer.

Angry words were shouted in German. The Hessians were coming—fierce German soldiers hired by the British.

Benjamin knew the Hessians preferred to kill rather than take prisoners. During the battle for Long Island, they'd bayoneted surrendering American soldiers.

Benjamin led Highlander down the slope. He and his men shoved the boat back into the river. Benjamin coaxed Highlander on board, then scuttled behind.

They set off, navigating across the strong current.

Cries from the Hessians were nearer still.

Several hundred Hessian soldiers appeared at the ferry—they were too late.

The boat was well on its way.

First, the Germans fired their muskets. Failing to hit the boat, they fired their cannons. Three-pound and six-pound cannonballs flew at Benjamin and his crew. They fell short, splashing into the river.

Benjamin inhaled a glorious breath of relief. He patted Highlander. They were safe.

Also safe was the American army, which had escaped to fight another day without losing a single man.

In the history of warfare I do not recollect a more fortunate retreat.
—Benjamin Tallmadge

*Our Retreat was made without any loss of Men or Ammunition
and in better order than I expected, from Troops in the Situation ours were. . . .*
—George Washington's letter to Congress following the retreat

Experiencing the strength and brutality of the British and narrowly escaping from Long Island made Benjamin Tallmadge even more of a patriot. He was promoted to captain on December 14, 1776, and appointed head of a troop of light dragoons, an esteemed position.

He knew he'd found a new career.

The dragoons were regiments in which all the men rode horses. Benjamin continued to ride Highlander. He commanded that all the horses in his troop be dapple-gray, like Highlander, and took pride in how superb they looked with black straps and black bearskin holster covers.

Benjamin went on to become the man George Washington trusted to organize and run his Culper Spy Ring. Appointed Washington's chief of secret service, Benjamin recruited agents in his hometown—Setauket, Long Island—and in New York City. The Culper Ring provided Washington with crucial information through-out the rest of the war.

Benjamin also remained in combat. Using whaleboats to cross Long Island Sound, he led his regiment on several successful surprise raids from American-held Connecticut to British-occupied Long Island. In his most celebrated raid, Tallmadge and his men destroyed British Fort St. George without losing the life of one American soldier. He received praise from Washington and from Congress for his efforts.

His distinguished military career included two more promotions during the war, to major and colonel.

After the war he became a successful businessman in Litchfield, Connecticut. He continued his dedication to his country as a congressman, serving in the House of Representatives from 1801 to 1817.

Benjamin married and wrote a memoir for his family. His words also proved important to his country, then and now. His is the story of a patriot and hero—a man who never acted for personal glory, but only for the glory of his nation.

1754 Benjamin Tallmadge is born in Setauket, Long Island, the second son of the Rev. Benjamin Tallmadge and Susannah Smith Tallmadge. There will be a total of five sons in the family.

1768 Benjamin's mother dies.

1769 In autumn, at age fifteen, Benjamin enters Yale College in Connecticut.

1773 Tallmadge graduates from Yale and speaks at his commencement. He immediately accepts an appointment as superintendent of the high school in Weathersfield, Connecticut.

1775 In April, the battles of Lexington and Concord take place. The Battle of Breed's Hill follows in June.

1776 On June 20, Tallmadge enlists in the army as lieutenant.
On July 4, the Declaration of Independence is adopted. The war officially begins.
On August 27, the Battle of Long Island is fought.
On September 16, the British defeat Washington's troops at the Battle of Harlem Heights.
On December 14, Tallmadge is promoted to captain. He commands a troop of light dragoons.
On December 25, Washington and his men cross the Delaware River. The next day they capture Trenton, New Jersey.

1777 On January 3, Washington wins the Battle of Princeton in New Jersey.
From January 6 until May 28, Washington and his troops winter in Morristown, New Jersey.
On April 7, Tallmadge is promoted to major.
On October 17, American troops defeat the British at the Battle of Saratoga.
On December 19, Washington settles his troops at Valley Forge, Pennsylvania, for a brutal winter. They remain there until June 19, 1778.

1778 On June 28, Washington fights the British to a draw at the Battle of Monmouth.
In August, at Washington's request, Tallmadge organizes and heads (under Washington) the Culper Spy Ring. The ring proves so useful that it continues for the rest of the war.

1780 Tallmadge leads three whaleboat raids from American-held Connecticut to British-held Long Island. Washington and Congress thank Tallmadge and his men.

1781 On October 19, British General Cornwallis surrenders at Yorktown, Virginia.

1783 On September 3, the Treaty of Paris is signed. The eight-year war is over.
On September 30, Tallmadge is promoted to colonel.
On December 4, Washington bids farewell to his troops at Fraunces Tavern in New York. Tallmadge later writes the only surviving record of that historic occasion.

1784 On March 18, Tallmadge marries Mary Floyd, daughter of William Floyd, a signer of the Declaration of Independence. The ceremony is conducted by Tallmadge's father. The couple settles in Litchfield, Connecticut, where Tallmadge becomes a successful businessman. They have five sons and two daughters.

1800 Tallmadge is elected to the House of Representatives and serves until 1817.

1805 Mary Floyd Tallmadge dies.

1808 Tallmadge marries Maria Hallett.

1812 President Madison invites Tallmadge to rejoin the army in a prominent position. He declines.

1835 On March 7, Benjamin Tallmadge dies at 81.

1858 Tallmadge's memoir is published posthumously.

Bronx, New York

Valentine-Varian House—3266 Bainbridge Avenue. Site of six skirmishes between American troops and the British forces who occupied the house for most of the Revolutionary War.

Van Cortlandt House—Van Cortlandt Park, Broadway at West 246th Street. Site of numerous military encampments by both the Americans and the British. Washington set up headquarters in the house in 1776 and again in 1783. For much of the war, Van Cortlandt House sat in "no-man's land"—in territory between the British in New York City and American troops to the north.

Brooklyn, New York

Battle Hill—In Greenwood Cemetery, 500 25th Street. A statue of Minerva, the Roman goddess of war, stands by an Altar to Liberty monument to mark the Battle of Long Island at this hill, where fighting actually occurred. Minerva faces out over the New York harbor, looking the Statue of Liberty in the eye.

Battle Pass—In Prospect Park, near the Brooklyn Museum. A stone monument marks this spot, where the Hessians launched their attack in the Battle of Long Island.

Fulton Ferry Landing (formerly Brooklyn Ferry)—At the foot of Old Fulton Street, on the East River. At this boat landing you can see the watery mile where Washington crossed his troops to safety. There is a boulder with a memorial plaque that commemorates the feat. Read Washington's inspirational words to his troops, engraved along the pier.

Old Stone House Historic Interpretive Center—In Byrne Park, Fourth Avenue and Third Street. This small house is a replica of the one used by a Maryland regiment to hold back the attacking British so that much of the American army could escape to Brooklyn Heights, at the sacrifice of 90 percent of the regiment. Today the house is a museum.

Long Island, New York

Earle-Wightman House—20 Summit Street, Oyster Bay. Housing the Oyster Bay Historical Society, this site features a one-room house from colonial times.

East Hampton Public Library, The Long Island Collection—159 Main Street, East Hampton. Excellent source for researching the Revolutionary period on Long Island.

Raynham Hall Museum—20 West Main Street, Oyster Bay. The Townsend family homestead was the site of British headquarters in Oyster Bay during the Revolutionary War. Little did the British know that one member of the Townsend family was also Washington's most trusted spy.

Rock Hall Museum—199 Broadway, Lawrence; Sands-Willets House—336 Port Washington Boulevard, Port Washington. Dating back to the early 1700s, these houses now serve as museums.

Stony Brook Grist Mill—Harbor Road, off Main Street, Stony Brook. The George Washington Spy Ring Interactive Kiosk.

Manhattan, New York

Fraunces Tavern Museum—54 Pearl Street. Site where Washington gave his farewell address to his troops in 1783. The tavern also served as a meeting place for pre-Revolutionary activities. Read Benjamin Tallmadge's description of Washington's farewell, on permanent display, along with interesting memorabilia from the war as well as changing exhibitions on Revolutionary War themes.

Morris-Jumel Mansion—65 Jumel Terrace. Washington's headquarters in September and October of 1776. Later used by the British.

About the Research and Writing Process . . .

History is not an exact science. We learn about the past from observations. No two people note the same details or experience an ordeal the same way. One remembers eating raw pork; another recalls the smell of gunpowder. The history writer is like an archeologist. He must dig through primary sources for fragments in time. He must piece them together, creating a vivid picture full of scent and sound. He must make history live.

I used Benjamin Tallmadge's memoir as the main source for this account. To get a complete feel for the period and the battle, I consulted every record I could find on Tallmadge and the times—letters and accounts of soldiers on both sides at the scene, George Washington's correspondence and records from the late 1700s, and newspaper accounts from the *Pennsylvania Gazette* and *Rivington's New York Loyal Gazette*, for example. To verify sources and find out more details, I visited sites, attended lectures, and contacted historians who were experts on Tallmadge, the period, and the battle.

Still, some points can never be pinned to certainty. Can I prove Tallmadge's horse whinnied at a precise moment? I cannot. But I know that horse was the beloved animal of a gentle man. I know horses spook easily in frightening situations, and this horse had never experienced battle. I've made an educated guess that the horse whinnied.

What is the truth? When studying history we rely on the memories of people like us. There will always be disagreements. We must trust our instincts and common sense to help us resolve them.

About Highlander's Name . . .

Sometimes a story just hits you. That's what happened when I came across Benjamin Tallmadge's account of the Battle of Long Island and how he went back for his horse. Bam! It struck me as I read it. *There* was a moment in history.

One problem: Tallmadge never mentioned the horse's name. Here's how I arrived at Highlander.

After the war, Tallmadge wrote about a horse he purchased for breeding named Brown Highlander. He wrote, "Highlander was a horse of fine size and symmetry, probably a better horse than his gray namesake." That meant that Highlander was named after a previous horse. I knew that the horse Tallmadge rescued was his favorite. Wouldn't he use his favorite horse as a namesake? I also knew that the horses in Tallmadge's dragoons were dapple-gray. The dragoons were formed soon after the Battle of Long Island, so I was sure that Tallmadge was using the same horse. I concluded that the original Highlander was Tallmadge's horse in 1776.

I asked an expert on the Revolution for his opinion. He wrote, ". . . I believe that your supposition is entirely plausible and probably the truth. I would feel comfortable using that name for Tallmadge's horse." So I did. —S.C.

The Author Would Like to Thank the Following for Their Expertise . . .

Amy Northrop Adamo, director,
Fraunces Tavern Museum, New York, New York
Bob Allegretto, Second Regiment Light Dragoons
(Tallmadge's troop)
Andrew Batten, former director of Fraunces Tavern
Museum and former executive director of Raynham
Hall Museum
Dr. Gary Corrado, author and historian,
Revolutionary War period
Catherine Fields, executive director,
Litchfield Historical Society, Litchfield, Connecticut
Brian Heinz, reenactor and enthusiast, Revolutionary
War period
Greg Johnson, research assistant,
David Library of the American Revolution,
Washington Crossing, Pennsylvania
Staff of the Abbot Public Library,
Marblehead, Massachusetts
Beverly Tyler, Long Island historian,
Three Village Historical Society, Setauket, New York

The Battle of Long Island

Primary Source

Tallmadge, Benjamin. *Memoir of Col. Benjamin Tallmadge*. New York: Thomas Holman, Book and Job Printer, corner of Centre and White Streets, 1858.

Additional Valuable Sources

Atlee, Samuel John. *Col. Atlee's Journal of the Battle of Long Island*. Harrisburg, PA: Excerpts from Pennsylvania Archives, 2nd series, Vol.1, 1874.

Billias, George Athan. *General John Glover and His Marblehead Mariners*. New York: Henry Holt and Company, 1960.

Burg, David F. *The American Revolution: An Eyewitness History*. New York: Facts on File, Inc., 2001.

Cifaldi, Susan L. *Benjamin Clark's Drum Book, 1797*. USA: The Hendrickson Group, 1989.

Commager, Henry Steele, and Richard B. Morris, eds. *The Spirit of 'Seventy-Six: The Story of the American Revolution as Told by Participants*. New York: Harper & Row, 1958.

Field, Thomas W. *The Battle of Long Island: With Preceding and Subsequent Events*. Brooklyn: Long Island Historical Society, 1869.

Force, Peter. *American Archives*. 5th Series, I. Valuable primary source material compiled; accounts by participants of the battle and evacuation.

Graydon, Alexander. *Memoirs of His Own Time*. Philadelphia: Lindsay & Blakiston, 1846.

Hall, Charles Swain. *Benjamin Tallmadge: Revolutionary Soldier and American Businessman*. New York: AMS Press, Inc., 1966.

Higgins, Charles M. *Brooklyn's Neglected Battle Ground*. New York: Witter and Kintner, 1910.

Ingram, Scott. *The Battle of Long Island*. Farmington Hills, MI: Blackbirch Press, 2004.

Johnston, Henry P. *The Campaign of 1776 Around New York and Brooklyn*. New York: DaCapo Press, 1971.

Long Island: Our Story. New York: Newsday, 1998.

Lowell, Edward J. *The Hessians*. New York: Harper & Brothers, 1884.

Manders, Eric I. *The Battle of Long Island*. Monmouth Beach, NJ: Philip Freneau Press, 1978.

Onderdonk, Henry, Jr. *Revolutionary Incidents of Suffolk and Kings Counties.* Port Washington, NY: Kennikat Press, 1849.

Rosengarten, J. G. *The German Allied Troops in the North American War of Independence, 1776–1783.* Albany, NY: Joel Munsell's Sons, 1893.

Stevenson, Charles Goldsmith. *The Battle of Long Island: "The Battle of Brooklyn."* Brooklyn: Brooklyn Bicentennial Commission, 1975.

Upham, William P. *Memoir of General John Glover, of Marblehead.* Salem, MA: Charles W. Swasey, 1863.

Articles

Chadwick, John W. "The Battle of Long Island." *Harper's New Monthly Magazine,* August 1876.

Myers, J. Jay. "George Washington's Dire Straits." *American History Magazine,* June 2001.

Wallace, John J. "Early Horse-History of Orange County." *Wallace's Monthly,* May 1876. Account of Highlander's pedigree, clue to horse's name.

Newspapers (Primary Sources)

Pennsylvania Gazette, 1776–1780. Read transcript at David Library, Washington Crossing, Pennsylvania.

Rivington's New York Loyal Gazette and *The Royal Gazette,* 1776–1780. Read on microfilm at David Library, Washington Crossing, Pennsylvania.

Additional Sources

The Abbot Public Library, Marblehead, Massachusetts
Brooklyn Public Library, Brooklyn, New York
The David Library of the American Revolution, Washington Crossing, Pennsylvania
The DeWint House, Tappan, New York
The East Hampton Public Library, East Hampton, Long Island

This pencil sketch of Benjamin Tallmadge in his dragoon's uniform was printed in his memoir. It was drawn by Colonel John Trumbull, a well-known American artist.

Fraunces Tavern Museum, New York, New York
Litchfield Historical Society, Litchfield, Connecticut
Marblehead Historical Society, Marblehead, Massachusetts
New-York Historical Society, New York, New York
The New York Public Library, New York, New York
The Old 76 House, Tappan, New York
The Oyster Bay Historical Society, housed in the Earle-Wightman House Museum, Oyster Bay, Long Island
Raynham Hall Museum, Oyster Bay, Long Island
Tappan Historical Society
Three Village Historical Society, Setauket, Long Island
Washington's Headquarters, Morristown, New Jersey

Additional Acknowledgments

Further thanks to Aunt Olga, Kent Brown Jr., Tony Castrovilla, Mom, Mom C., Nancy Feldman, Margaret "Bunny" Gabel, Pascale LaForest, Reid Mihalko, the Graduate Writing Program at The New School, and Long Island Children's Writers and Illustrators (with special gratitude to my mentors, Brian Heinz and Orel Protopopescu).

About the Art Research . . .

I conduct my research by visiting libraries, historical sites, and costume shops. I photograph friends and family as my models. I refer to books, videos, and photographs from my own collection.

For *By the Sword*, my artwork was reviewed by Amy Northrop Adamo of Fraunces Tavern Museum; Gary Corrado, historian; and Brian Heinz, reenactor, to make sure it was accurate.

The time spent on research can take longer than actually painting the pictures. I paint in oils on linen canvases.

—B.F.

Designs from the Colonial Period . . .

Although America was struggling to break free from Great Britain at this time, the most common typographical font used in printing was designed by an Englishman, William Caslon, in the early 1700s. Ironically, both the U.S. Constitution and the Declaration of Independence were set with his font. This book uses the fonts Adobe Caslon for its text and Caslon BE Expert for its numbers. It is a font that is known for its beauty and readability.

—C.P.

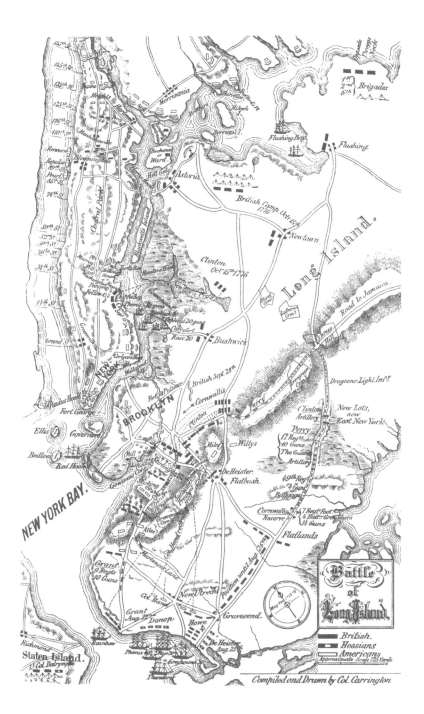

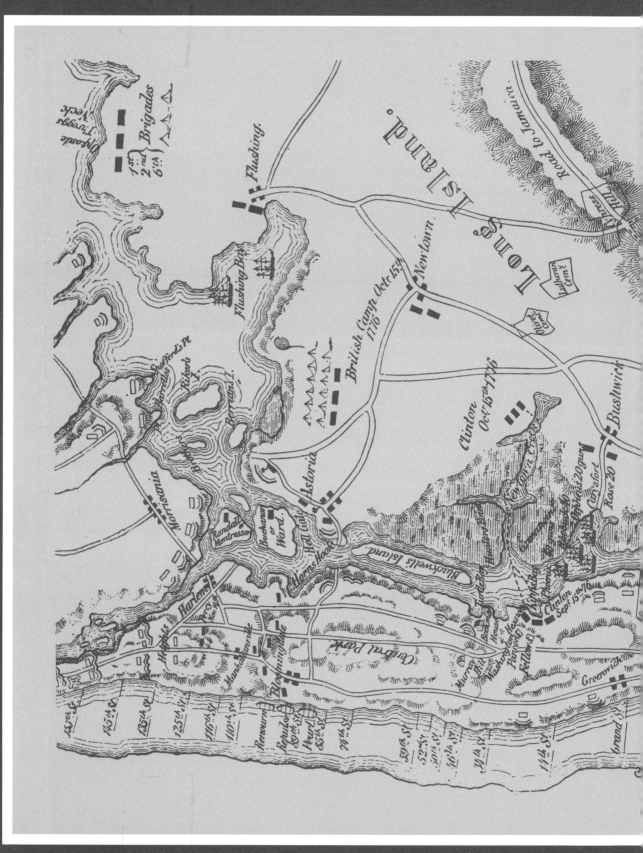